Second Story Sally

MEG CARAHER

ILLUSTRATED BY LEIGH HOBBS

Published by
Sundance Publishing
33 Boston Post Road West
Suite 440
Marlborough, MA 01752
800-343-8204
www.sundancepub.com

Copyright © text Meg Caraher
Copyright © illustrations Leigh Hobbs
Project commissioned and managed by
Lorraine Bambrough-Kelly, The Writer's Style
Designed by Cath Lindsey/design rescue

First published 1997 by
Addison Wesley Longman Australia Pty Limited
95 Coventry Street
South Melbourne 3205 Australia
Exclusive United States Distribution: Sundance Publishing

ISBN 978-0-7608-1931-9

Printed by Nordica International Ltd.
Manufactured in Guangzhou, China
August, 2015
Nordica Job#: CA21501102
Sundance/Newbridge PO#: 228178

Contents

For my Mom, Marion,
who loved to read . . .
And for my Dad, George,
who loves to write.

Chapter 1

The Professional

"No moon tonight. Just the way I like it," whispered ten-year-old Second Story Sally, flexing her fingers inside her leather gloves.

She pulled down her velvet mask and crept through the ivy. Parting the leaves, she took hold of the drainpipe.

Silently, winding arms and legs up and around the pipe, she shimmied up to the pitch-black second story.

Once inside, she paused, listening.

All quiet. The house slept.

Slinking, creeping, silent as a cat, Second
Story Sally (or Triple S as she was
sometimes known) moved downstairs into
the study. By the beam of her flashlight,
she saw what she was after—the safe!

She pounced.

Underneath her black mask, her eyes glittered with excitement. She loaded up her bag with strings of pearls, diamond rings, and stacks of money.

Slinging the bag of loot onto her back, she stiffened. Was that a noise? Would a police car come screaming up to the house at any minute?

Triple S didn't hang around to find out.

Chapter 2

The Schoolgirl

"How did it go, Sally, hon — I mean, Second Story Sally?" asked Mom. She watched as her daughter flung the loot onto the kitchen counter and poured herself a glass of orange juice.

"Any problems?" asked her Dad, who was eating bacon and eggs for breakfast.

"Easy-peasy," said Second Story Sally, smiling.

She peeled off her black velvet bodysuit and slipped into her school clothes. Now she was back to being schoolgirl Sally.

"But I'm afraid Mr. Big won't be happy. It's back to the drawing board for his new state-of-the-art Big's Burglar Alarm System," Sally explained.

"Only one more job and you'll have the money for the stray cat shelter," reminded Dad.

"And a vacation!" exclaimed Sally.

Sally's parents looked at her in astonishment. Sally nodded her head at them proudly.

"Mr. Big said there'd be a bonus for me once I had tested the new batch of alarms. So I thought I'd take us on a vacation when school gets out."

"But, Sally, you've been so generous already. It's because of your money that we were able to build the second story onto our house," Dad explained.

"Yes, but you two gave me my very first kitten. And he taught me nearly everything I know about being as quiet as a mouse. By the way, where *is* Chas?"

"Usual place. Upstairs, curled up asleep in the shower stall," Mom smiled. "That cat is weird, Sally. Someone should tell him cats are supposed to like warm, cozy places."

"Oh, he does. In winter. But in summer he loves the feel of cold tiles against his fur. I'd better go upstairs and say good-bye to him," said Sally.

"Hurry up, honey, you don't want to be late for school. And don't forget you've got to go and see Mr. Big this afternoon and return the jewels," reminded Mom.

Chapter 3

Mr. Big Has a Problem

In his laboratory, Mr. Benjamin Big scratched his head and blinked anxiously at the girl in the black velvet bodysuit.

"How am I going to solve the problem with my alarm, Second Story Sally? It should have activated as soon as you entered the mansion," he explained.

"I wish I could help you, Mr. Big. I'm good at breaking and entering, and I'm a great cat burglar, but alarms . . . sorry."

"I must be missing something with the lab testing. The alarm is not sensitive enough. Perhaps I need to . . . "

"I've got it!" cried Second Story Sally. "Cats! They are silent and fast and light on their feet. If your alarm can catch a cat, it can catch a burglar! It needs to be tested with real cats. All sorts of real cats."

"Great idea, Triple S, but where am I going to get my hands on all sorts of real cats at a moment's notice?" asked Mr. Big.

Second Story Sally lifted up her mask and gave him a wink and a smile.

She had cat friends everywhere, just waiting to be gainfully employed in return for a gourmet fish dinner.

And Mr. Big did just what she suggested. He tested his alarm system with fat cats, tall cats, striped cats, and skinny cats. He tested and retested with long cats, fluffy cats, black cats, and tomcats.

And finally, he was ready!

The Bells Go Off!

In the deep, black, middle of the night, Second Story Sally entered the biggest mansion in the neighborhood.

She knew what she had to do—turn off the alarm system without alerting anybody and make her way to the antique china cabinet.

Suddenly she heard a deafening sound.
Er Ree, Er Ree, Er Ree, Er Ree!

Yes! It worked! Mr. Big's Burglar Alarm
System finally worked!

Mr. and Mrs. Collins burst out of their bedroom and flicked on the light in the living room. In rushed Mr. Big in his striped pajamas!

"They let me stay overnight for the alarm test," explained Mr. Big to a startled Second Story Sally.

Second Story Sally stayed for a small celebration before Mr. Big drove her through the sleeping neighborhood to her own home. Clutched in her hand was the cash bonus he'd promised.

"You've been so valuable to my business, Triple S. I know you'll be busy with the stray cat shelter, but if you ever want to go back to the cat burglar profession, let me know," said Mr. Big.

"Thanks, Mr. Big. I'll let you know."
Second Story Sally lifted up her mask and
gave him a wink and a smile.

Slinking up the driveway to her house,
Triple S decided against using the front door
and crept around to the back of the house.

"Once more, for old time's sake," she
whispered to herself, taking hold of the
drainpipe and heaving herself up. Up, up,
up she went, higher and higher, toward her
bedroom window on the second story.

Suddenly she froze.

Chapter 5

The Cat and the Burglar

Her bedroom window was open. She knew she had left it closed.

Second Story Sally got such a shock she lost her grip and started to fall.

She desperately clamped her arms and legs around the drainpipe and held on tightly, breathing hard.

Trembling with fright, she inched her way back up to the window and peeked in.

What if someone was hiding in the dark, waiting for her? Should she call out for Mom and Dad? But what if she frightened the intruder and he or she panicked and tried to push her out the window?

"Oh, what am I going to do?" she asked herself, jiggling up and down on the drainpipe in agitation, hoping to shake out an idea.

And she did.

As quietly as she could, Second Story Sally climbed through the window into her bedroom and closed it behind her.

She crept through the darkness, out of her bedroom, past the bathroom, past the guest room, and downstairs to the kitchen.

Quietly, she picked up the telephone and shone her tiny flashlight on the numbers. She dialed the police.

She whispered her name and address urgently and hoped that the burglar was not hiding in the kitchen.

But as she put the phone down and switched off the flashlight, she heard a soft thud from the living room.

Second Story Sally jumped with fright and fell against the kitchen counter, sending the glass fruit bowl crashing to the kitchen floor.

She screamed as she heard footsteps going upstairs, and shouted out in fear, "MOM! DAD!" and then started frantically turning on lights.

"What's wrong, Sally, hon—I mean Second Story Sally?" called Mom anxiously.

"Someone . . . in . . . up . . . stairs," she gulped, pointing upstairs.

"He could be hiding in any of the rooms. Or he might have escaped. It'll be hard to find him."

"MEEOWW! MEEOWW! MEEOWW! MEEOWW!"

"It's Chas!" cried Dad.

The whole family raced upstairs.

There, cornered in the shower, guarded by
a growling, hissing Chas . . .

was the burglar.

Just at that moment, there was a loud knock on the front door. "Police!"

"I'll get the door," offered Second Story Sally.

"No, they'll arrest *you*, silly. You're still in your work clothes. I'll go," said Mom, looking at Second Story Sally in her black velvet bodysuit.

Upstairs in the bathroom, the police questioned and arrested one badly scratched burglar.

"It's high time we got a burglar alarm for our house," Dad commented.

"You've got plenty of connections in that area, Sally, hon—I mean Second Story Sally. Got any ideas?" joked Mom.

"I'm sure Mr. Big and I will be able to come to some arrangement!" Second Story Sally lifted up her mask and gave her parents a wink and a smile.

Meg Caraher

Meg lives in a suburb of Melbourne, Australia, with her husband Maurice, daughter Stephanie, and their Burmese cat, Binnie Noo Noo.

Meg started writing novels for fun when she was ten. At the age of seventeen she won a scholarship as an exchange student in the United States. After her return to Australia, Meg attended the National Theatre School of Drama, in St. Kilda.

Although for many years writing took a back seat, Meg is now studying for a Diploma of Arts in Professional Writing and Editing. She has won a poetry competition and received two short story awards. Second Story Sally is her second novel for children.

About the Illustrator

Leigh Hobbs

Leigh Hobbs paints and creates sculptures, but he enjoys drawing most of all. He has illustrated a number of children's books, including *Mr. Knuckles* and *Old Tom* (which he also wrote). Often, you will see Leigh's cartoons in the Melbourne, Australia, newspaper, the *Age*.

Leigh lives in the suburb of Melbourne known as Williamstown.